BAD

The Party Skunks of the South Bay

When the conventions come to town there's chicken sometimes, sandwich shards among the square planters and the white-trunked ficus, reflecting pools that reflect and colored jets that fling chlorine drops of amethyst and amber. Maybe it's the disinfectants or whatever they're feeding the chicken, but we can't think in a straight line. The skunks totter past, delicate and soft-limbed, but get closer and it's evident there's something wrong with those girls. Raccoon, they used to say, back when they could still make jokes, Raccoon, go down to Belmont Pier and tell me those aren't plastic bags in the water, and we've forgotten now why that seemed so funny at the time. Considering our position, we've concluded, we're unusually sensitive to current events. We've tried a lot of strategies and gone so far as to hire consultants and sit through day-long webinars, but they make less sense every time and we've started to believe all kinds of things about ourselves, we've started to feel something in common with what we formerly derided. There are the pathetic grannies of varied ethnicities and low startle points who collect themselves to cross the big intersections as if they're heading out to sea, there are the sellers of oranges and roses at offramps.

Raccoon Gets His Feelings Hurt
He disappears into the storm drain, almost too fat to fit, when the headlights sweep by. He grins, wide and sly. Raccoon considers himself a product of nature, but like the rest of us he's dizzied by something, maybe the insecticide-soaked cockroaches he throws down like peanuts every night. He keeps company with the worst kinds of feral cats, the addled possums and insomniac mockingbirds of three in the morning. All afternoon he sleeps in a tree and

farts like a real degenerate. That's his problem, no follow-through, and we tried to manage, to work around it, but eventually we had to say something because when someone is that important to the whole operation, when no one else can make sense of the latest e-mail from Human Resources or the fine print on the 401K, we'd rather risk some hurt feelings if it means keeping the usual victims from doing the usual flat-on-the-asphalt victim thing. Raccoon responds when we run him down behind his back, he's no \ idiot, he gets this expression on his face, his put-upon smarmy look, and there's some fear, too, because as we pointed out, Raccoon isn't one hundred percent himself.

Things Were Fine, Then It All Went To Hell
We lived how we could, below the berms and on the traffic Ys. Fragile stalks of wild radish supported our cocoons. We breathed diesel exhaust through the silken bundle, and then one day we burst through. This place is no stranger to bucket and blade, the dregs of cement from the hopper, tailings of asphalt. Rules exist, but they can't cover everything, no fair to expect that they'll answer every question, what shall we do with this? Dump it in the weeds, the rain will wash it away, draw it down to the aquifer, capillary action.

Crisis Mode
Whatever blew ashore sent the seagulls inland where they amuse themselves in the usual way, wheel over the

Eastland Mall and the thousands of naked bears clutching the wheels in their purring boxes. We creatures of habit and habitat under mackerel cloud and frail palms spray whitewash on the weeds, we shake the empties behind the Serbian Brotherhood and line up for a handout at St. Mary Star of the Sea. The truth is that Raccoon and all those cats are a real problem, more trouble than help some days, they make all of us look bad by shitting and getting into things, but much as we try to escape it we always agree to collective guilt around here, guilt by association, the blurred composite on the wanted poster, a dozen traumatized witnesses. We take comfort in this: it's still a civil society, nobody crowbars up the sidewalks to pave their patios, and when some enterprising bandit steals the pipes or the wire to sell for scrap they do it in a seemly manner, they dress the part, like electricians and plumbers, they have a clipboard and a counterfeit work order and check in at the front desk. After things go dark or the puddles spread, the "out of order" signs appear on clean paper, eye level and square-jawed, and we all feel awe at how well things are going, even the frauds and the disasters get a protocol, the corruption and the unforeseen outcomes have a staff and a budget.

Who Gets The Bees?
There aren't as many of them, and on our bad days we start to think the illusion of competence is just that, that no one gets it, no one sees how everything eventu-

ally comes back to us, conversations and old newspapers, what breaks down and what holds up. Nobody leaves early so the staff can clean up properly, no one considers how they're fouling the nests, the accidents to come that will shred the protocols, no one denies the potential of the unseemly, of context ripped away and thrown to the wind.

Vertical-Horizontal Illusions
The danger here is perspective, its loss, and people in business casual, blond and dark, their mouths set in a certain expression. If our perspective holds up we could comfort ourselves that they gather here disproportionate to their true numbers, the women in closeout heels and the men in khaki pants who say things into the mobile phones, to bosses, to co-workers, to wives and boyfriends and children, especially to the children, things that leave us wondering at the ways of the world, at how a person can say for instance, "I'm very disappointed in you" when there are tears audible through the headpiece, how a kid's soccer game can be a crucible, an ordeal, a test the father judges like Zeus on his throne, forgetting the sodden fields and chilled fingers of his own sad youth. What surprised us all was how the two-legged kids could melt Raccoon, especially if they put on one of those animal hats with fake mouse ears or panda markings. Raccoon sat in his storm drain and we watched the anger just drain out of him, someone could drop a

breakfast burrito right between his paws and he'd hardly notice.

We Have Materials For Which We Have No Forms
Mockingbird sings it all, but she's tired of telling the same story over and over, and it makes less sense every time. We don't know if Raccoon just got sick of it all and hopped a bus, or if there was something sinister, something to Mockingbird's hints about the parking-lot sweeper, the new sign that reads, "It's YOUR parking lot; let's keep it clean!" Mockingbird composes in her own way her own autistic blues of cement labyrinths, crushed kittens that look like tiny foxes from a horrified distance, the silent owls of fate. She's not nocturnal by nature, she suffers from insomnia in a way we can't understand, suffering as we do from so many things but never from our beloved stars and street lamps haloed in late-night fog. It's an urban life all right and it should be exciting, but they never warn you, Mockingbird, that survival is a habit like any other. Bad company at the edges, things that could go wrong so quickly—it's best to watch and sing and grab whatever flies by. What would we do if some real specialist showed up, a rare refugee with finicky tastes?

Vladimir Ilyich Lenin lives on La Brea
Or so we hear. His head lives there, at least, with Mao balancing atop. No one needs to remind us that the

political scene has shifted, the old verities have weakened and the entire world could hang on an oilfield in Mali or the disaffected youth of Brazil. We know we don't get the whole picture. Nocturnal types seldom do. What we see is this: we see young ladies in their party dresses, arm in arm or bedraggled and alone, waiting after the cocktail lounge goes dark. Look, they say into their phones, I know it's late, I wouldn't ask if I could call anyone else, and the ex-boyfriend or the sleepy girlfriend still wobbly from her own night out rolls up a few minutes later. We see the misalliances and missed connections, but we miss the resolution to go on, the young ladies arranging the post-its on their desks, watering the plants, checking the eggs for cracks.

Form Finds Its Material In Its Own Good Time
No one means any malice by it, but it's hard to see it as anything else. The trucks and bulldozers show up, blade the mustard and the wild radish, the sea heather and the chaparral, sink beams into the ground, rebar, block, deep foundations that puddle up in the winter rains. One after another they appear in white hard hats, trace their blue lines on rolled paper or consider more and more often the glowing blue screens of silver machines with half-eaten fruit on the lid, a bite extracted like Eve has been and gone. For the lizards among us, a pile of rocks means the world, a thicket of scrub is Mardi Gras for Mocking-bird. If we could find Raccoon, if we could bring him back

here, pay him whatever he asked, guilt him into helping
us, we'd issue a manifesto on what hatches and sprouts,
we'd ask you to leave it alone, we'd enumerate the fields
of grim deportation and the damp trails of mist, what's
really important, what disappears as the sun comes up,
the bonfire embers cool, the warning buoy hoots its last
across the bay.

COUGAR COMES OF AGE

I.

Cougar appears, a tawny stalker, to women walking early. They wave their arms and scream. It was crouched to spring, they tell the police, but how do they know?

Nervous and slandered, Cougar stalks the neighborhood, breaks through a window screen. Once inside, he doesn't know what to do. Bears and raccoons know: sample the breakfast cereal, shred the upholstery, terrorize the poodle. But the big cat stands resolute and four-footed, sniffing. Humanity fouls the air. What am I doing here, he wonders, what switch got tripped? Rocks I know, and dry creek beds, and endless stands of oak. No one can help him.

Down the road, they're blading the hills, shrouded now by summer's haze, and Cougar walks on, testing his mistake.

II.

On a bench by the duck pond, Cougar stretches his legs and looks around for snacks. Ducks are scarce, but he's still picking the aging Yorkie he had for dinner out of his back teeth. It's quiet. Only a dull thud from the freeway disturbs the night. Venus hangs in the western sky, and Cougar recalls fragments of his life as a kit, trotting downhill until Venus tangled herself in the ridgetop trees and disappeared. Back then, mountains could eat planets, but they're just smudges now, twinkles on the black northern sky. Not long ago his mother gave him a beating he thought would kill him, and he ran, puking and bleeding, through the culverts downstream. You'd better head to town, his mother said, one last bit of advice he'd take from her before he grew big enough to fight back.

But tawny fur hides scars aplenty, and he's smart enough now not to manifest, sitting at bus stops, baseball cap pulled low over his eyes. He smiles when the man on the next bench jabs at his newspaper and says "Have you ever seen one?" The naked bears are reading about him.

"They watch for loners. One bite to the back of the neck, and you're finished."

That sounds familiar. His mother again: Look for the unloved wanderer, the one no one will miss. And now, as his live-amber eyes scan the duck pond's green depths, Cougar wonders, doesn't that just about describe him? He looks around for the source of the gaze at the back of his neck.

III.

Cougar throws a party, but he's socially inept. Maybe it's the food: humans resembling bears so closely, he serves up mounds of fish and half-rotted berries, and pours warm pond-water with a liberal hand. Then there's the music—all he has are old 78s. At least he got the dance floor right, thanks to his rustic tastes. It's smooth wood, right up to the walls. But the crowd scattered early by Cougar's standards, and now everyone's gone.

In the corner, a gramophone pops and clicks, and Cougar sits mesmerized by a green lava lamp. My, but he's haunted by his kithood. Outside an isolated single-wide at the end of the road, Cougar and his twin sibling (dead now, certainly) watched the caretaker for the church camp. He brought in stacks of videos every

Sunday night, when buses and vans had gone. Pop! Crack! Boom! On went the manufactured wars, as moon rose and coyotes rustled dry heaps of leaves.

That was the only road Cougar ever saw, a thin patchwork of broken asphalt, until now. Now, the wide strips of gray cement take the crowds away, so efficient, so melancholy. Next time, streamers, one of those bouncy castles with a noisy blower. Maybe some crayfish or owl pellets. He should have got out more as a kit, visited the churchly folk, peeped into the dining hall windows to see what the naked bears were eating, put his head into that noose of golden, golden light.

IV.

Cougar's not looking his best: too many late nights. But he feels the itch and asks Coyote to fix him up with the orange tabby behind the Dairy Queen. They trot dark streets, Coyote and Cougar, Cougar lost in dreams, Coyote wondering if she should speak up, say what's on her mind. That tabby, for example. She'll act interested, but Cougar is too big for her, too much cat. She'll keep you in suspense, Cougar, then vanish, spread lies, say I've eaten her. Why should she be different from all the rest of her breed? Besides, why do you think she's so sleek and fat? Coyote's dying to say it: That one's never had a litter, someone's had her fixed. You'll yip and yowl to no effect.

You'd just as well do it with me.

Did she say it aloud? There's no talking to Cougar

about breaking the cross-genus taboo. He's not yet so debased. He wants a cat, even a stripped-down domestic model. Coyote sighs, a big sigh, ruffling the fur on Cougar's flank. He's always a step ahead. Cougar's a difficult companion, picky, forever hungry. Coyote tries to expand his horizons, tips over a garbage can, noses a dead rat from under a privet-hedge. It hasn't been dead long. She tosses it in the air to tempt him, and Cougar feels the wave of memory push at his back, locks his knees to stay in place. Coyote isn't doing herself much good here. Just like a canid, clever but too eager.

They've wasted a night, anyway. The tabby's gone, living with a cross-country trucker who spoils her with carne asada and beer in saucers. Other strays at the dumpster pass on the news, hoping for a sign of regard, but they don't interest Cougar. They seem so cloudy-brained and deferential. The tabby, with her slow-blinking green eyes, had something, something predatory. He imagined her nape a solid mouthful between his teeth, her eyes narrowed to involuntary slits.

V.

Silly Cougar, he could have his pick. One of the women he surprised in the park, for example, can't stop thinking about him. There was something sexual about that cat, or maybe it was just nearly dying. Her husband grunts in his sleep, but she's been awake for hours, straining for the scent of pine, dust in her teeth. She's heard that boy cats have barbs, that's why it's so noisy. Maybe it's a dream, where she's howling from her gut, immobilized by pain: sleep at last, the best outcome, unbarbed, unchafed by fur.

Her husband waits until her breathing deepens, then slips out of bed and out the door. He's thinking of Goethe, he's playing contrapuntal scales on his palm, he's walking the streets, breathing damp eucalyptus. Cougar, fast asleep on a slippery bough, drops behind him like a stone into water, but the man, deep in the German Enlightenment, walks on.

VI.

Morning. Cougar watches the sun rise over the tile roofs. All this could have been his, miles of sage and chamise brittle with drought, dried to dun and dark copper.

He crouches lower, nose to dusty tire tracks. The bozos haven't come out yet to ride their buzzing machines, but they will, no matter how hot the day. For a long time, Cougar watches a human sit on a rock. He creeps closer. Is there no place to get away from them, no place where they won't tempt his appetites?

The human takes a bit of watermelon from a bowl, holds it for a minute like a sacrament. She drops it in the dust and the ants at her feet swarm the fruit. More boil up from a funnel-shaped hole in the dust. She doesn't look up, but Cougar knows she knows he's there. Hairless ones, feeding ants. Now Cougar has seen everything. From where he crouches, he could crush her spine at the neck, drag her down a ravine, make a meal. Who would miss this antwoman? But Cougar stays in the weeds.

VII.

Later, he has doubts, regrets, even. It's been a few days. He's hungry. Lizards, a deaf or careless dog, baby possums, who can live on a diet like that? Romping kittens and overfed housetoms roam the gullies, but he won't touch those, and the slow, stupid ducks must sense him a mile off. They're molting and nervous. Red-tails perched on street lights flare the game if they see Cougar on a stalk, brushing the sage with their raptor's shadow, just for spite, and the ravens don't even bother to take wing when he slides by. He's lethargic, his fur is falling out in clumps. Times like this, the soft-boned blond children in the subdivisions could start to look good. There are so many of them. He crouches in a storm drain, amber eyes gleaming, and waits for the puff of breath at his flank, the companion he's come to expect, if not welcome.

"Do it," Coyote says. "I would if I could, but it's no good to kill if you can't drag. Besides, carrion's good enough for me. But you. They're going to shoot you anyway. You might as well go out with a full belly."

"Shoot me? Why would they bother?"

"Those women in the park. You didn't seem afraid of them."

"I wasn't afraid of them. What do you take me for?"

"No matter. Your mistake. You were doomed from the minute you locked eyes with those broads."

"So why do you hang around?"

"I can't help it." Coyote stifles a sob and farts instead—gas, the curse of the all-roadkill diet. "You are trouble for me. Don't I deserve something?"

So Cougar exerts himself, although he's sick with disgust. Afterward, Coyote, indiscriminate, lopes away to check the offramp for crushed fauna. Sex makes her hungry. But Cougar wants nothing more than to retreat to the highest peaks, above the tree line, and wait for a man in orange to take him out. There's no water this year, the deer are dying—but why wait in the flats for a functionary with a shotgun?

Post coitum, cat triste. Is that all? Cougar senses he's turned a corner, his code in tatters.

VII.

Most days he goes unnoticed, waiting in line for coffee, cracking peanuts at a minor-league game. Cougar's one of the crowd then, hairier than most, shy, polite to old people. Some days he smells a little musky. But tonight, astalk in the quiet cul-de-sacs, he's all cougar. Lately he's living on the edge, rubbing against trees, rattling the mailboxes, sending the neighborhood dogs into frenzies of barking. Everyone seems so nervous in the heat, imagining threatening whiffs of smoke. There's a newspaper on the front seat of a pickup truck and Cougar doesn't think twice before breaking the passenger-side window. He ignores the blood dripping on the seat and reads the headline that caught his eye. A bear somewhere has snagged himself a baby, taken that scary first step. Another story, way back on page five, mentions — at last! — Cougar. His foray into the house has won him fame. He will be drugged and relocated to a less populated place.

Sure. Back east, they've already shot the bear. Cougar tosses the bloodied newspaper back in the truck and trots off down the street. For a moment, he allows himself to hope. Wyoming, maybe, or New Mexico. Canada? All the best spots are taken. He watches his flanks. Better to take his chances here than wait to starve on herds of elk that aren't there.

VIII.

Cougar doesn't know it, but he's an aberration, an unusual cat. In the mountains, he'd only chase and sleep. A leaf, tossed in the wind, would stimulate his nerves to a painful pitch, and then he'd doze. But here in town, there are patterns to seek, customs to observe. Cougar perches on a ridge, and, recklessly exposed, watches the headlights sweep along the freeway, blend into the red brake lights ahead, do the same from the other direction. He can sit there for hours, but dusk is his favorite time. If the antwoman happens by, he's resolved to eat her, but she's elusive. He sneaks into backyards, hides under decks until the charcoal burns down, and then, as dark falls, he's so absorbed by human rituals that he forgets to steal the meat until it's cooked and ruined.

All this education has done is leave him hungry. He doesn't belong, but the forest seems dull by comparison. Somewhere far off there's the same baby owl screaming from its tree, the same droning crickets. Still, he's over-stimulated, not getting his twenty hours, and ever eying the slow blond children. He's sure to cross the line eventually, has already done it in his mind a hundred times. In the wild, he fumes, at least there are no moral decisions to make, no complex balance to strike between eating and pissing off the authorities.

The children ride by on indigestible bikes, climb on bright unappetizing plastic. Even that's a problem, even the clothes are a problem. It would be a laugh to finally get a square meal and then choke on a disposable diaper.

VIX.

Someone needs to save Cougar from himself. Coyote's no help. She's having a false pregnancy, and anyway, she's an instigator. If Cougar eats one of the naked bears, it'll make what she imagines she's carrying that much less grotesque. Or maybe more. She's confused. Her daily rounds are disrupted and the ravens eat what she misses, joke about how much she's slipped. How did they come to this?

Seeing Cougar in his favorite storm drain, Coyote affects a limp to draw sympathy and leaves herself exposed. A two-way radio squawks in the chaparral, and she panics, forgets to forget the imagined pain. Her stuttering run leads her in the bullet's path.

One paw shot clean off: now the limp is real.

X.

The naked bears think they've winged Cougar. They saw a flash of tawny fur, found a trail of blood. That'll lay some fear on him, they agree, and begin to relax. It's October now. In a week, or maybe two, it'll rain and dampen the rocks, put out the fires, wash clean the hybrid creature Coyote imagines she'll bring forth in the weeds.

A man in orange bags a hefty male atop a rocky draw, and Cougar's ears twitch with the echoing shot, two hundred miles away. He leaves the crowded bus at the next stop. It's time to cross the arroyos, claim the ridges, take the father's place. He'll get some sleep and expunge the crimes almost committed. It shouldn't be hard to find a real cat to love. Surely he can reform, live clean, adopt a healthy diet of baby deer and whatever hobbles by.

But he hasn't wasted his time. He's studied their habits, and one day they'll come to him—the trail-runners, the bird-watchers, the day-hikers. He won't manifest too soon. He'll keep to the shadows. One bite to the neck will prove that he's at last learned how to choose. His nervous symptoms will subside. Only sometimes, in his sleep,

will he travel, watch the freeways, haunt the bus stops
and the dreams of early-morning walkers, town-dwellers,
lovers of cats.

COYOTE IN WINTER

I.

Tailless and tripod, Coyote endured another January afternoon at the corner of Pico and Western. A glass-half-full type, she ignored her meager earnings for the day and focused on the light, decidedly pretty earlier, but now going gray, like the people milling about the bus stop. Sunday evening's a bad time to rely on mass transit, but Coyote considered the cyclical nature of existence and it calmed her. Some Januaries you ride the bus and some you have a Christmas tree on the curb waiting for the hauler to pick it up, but it's different times in your life, what under some lenses and in some lights you call the "good times" and the "bad times." It's having all these neighbors, twenty million of them, and all at a distance, that makes it hard to say for sure which is which.

And how would she define this time, as a good one or a bad one? Coyote never took a day off, and she traveled at a trot, wary of the thud and sigh and especially the folding doors of the bus, careful of her remaining extremities. Life did its lopping off, you couldn't stop it. How many others at the corner were here because of bad luck or love gone bad, how special could she call herself, anyway?

On the plus side, Coyote had a little cooker, a homemade thing on wheels, and spent her nights and weekends selling corn on the cob to customers who today were clumsy with cold, wasteful, dropping limes and rooster sauce and garlic salt on the sidewalk. She gave too much away, according to the last coyote she loved, and he should know. At least she had her kits out of the deal, with their accumulation of nights stowed away, sleeping and warm like money in the bank, acorns in the hollow tree, something to feel good about and balance out the debit column. By all objective measures she'd failed with them like most mothers fail, imposed the usual conflict-ing imperatives, tried to keep them home and at the same time pushed them to get out of the neighborhood, to deny the instinct to roam and mate, feed and howl. If failure was part of being a coyote, why should a coyote go beyond its coyote self? She'd lost plenty trying to answer that one. For a moment she let her mind wander to the one wild love of her life, the moments with the unequivocally savage Cougar, but it seemed a century ago.

Two ravens, fighting over a sack of cold fries, eyed her and flapped away.

"Rough night," one said to the other.

"For some I could name, they're all rough."

They could only mean her. Contemptuous as they seemed, ravens never poured quite so much scorn on the naked bears or other birds, the source of all good things: garbage and abandoned eggs, uncleared café tables and tender hatchlings. Ravens, those natural idolaters, rec-ognized Coyote as mortal like them, a consumer and not a producer, earthbound, doglike. In spite of Coyote's good nature, ravens bothered her, and on her bad days she felt the urge to spend some energy chasing one of them down, surprising it with her speed, and, canines to neck, bird-bones cracking under her weight, making it talk about what the big trash birds only suggested as they lazily took wing. Honesty like that could cripple them forever, but why should they be special? With her graying muzzle and matted coat, aching scars and phantom pains, Coyote felt the weight of her age and experience, the sudden blast of the gunshot and the lingering misery of a night spent gnawing at her own flesh. She had trouble understanding what it all meant, all this surviving. For a while it was being a mother, but now sometimes Coyote found herself slumped at the top of a stilled escalator on Wilshire, not hungry and not sleepy, idly tossing a mouse dazed by the fluorescent lights along the building's edge, as her offspring joined the great pack of whole coyotes and brought up kits of their own, unblemished, unmarked by events.

Tailless, tripod, scarred by love, Coyote lived in a world not of her own making, deriving small comforts from her memories and the almost imperceptible way each conscious moment veered from the ordinary. She always woke ready for a new day, at least. The Korean entrepreneurs who employed her part-time appreciated this very much, and when she opened the coffee stand each weekday morning, put out the bottles of soda and sweetened fruit juice, decanted the iced tea into the dispenser and arranged bagels and muffins under the plastic cover, she felt the unmistakable wave of satisfaction from a job well done. What did she have to compare it to? Most of her contemporaries were dead, roadkill on the way to wherever they planned to spend the next minute, pressed flat by the future. And their grandiosity still made her laugh, a rueful little bark that her grandkits knew meant she'd shaken off her gloom and would be good for a romp in a minute. How many coyotes crossed the freeway for a better life, sniffed the air for suggestions of prosperity, took up a risky residence in someone's garden shed and met their end at the hands of vector control? They drank the anti-freeze, ate the baited carcasses, aimed for the stars. For all her bloody stumps, Coyote had endured; for all the shame her kits felt at her deformity, they at least had a chance at a life like hers, an urban life of storm drains and sticky sidewalks, quick reflexes and realistic expectations.

II.

The dog had a watchful air, as dogs often do when on their own. He was bigger than Coyote, and older, too. She'd come to believe she could take any dog out, but this one would give her trouble, she could tell, especially at her age.

"Don't let the bulk fool you," he said. "I have a soft mouth. They got me for the kids, originally."

She tried to ignore him, but he hung out at the corner until late, then appeared at the coffee stand the next morning, curling up next to a chair on the sidewalk as if waiting for a latte-seeking owner. She had a busy shift, pulling espressos and bagging pastries, selling bus passes and newspapers, but the dog always kept himself in her sight-lines, and she came to admire his insouciant pose and to like his eyes as they sometimes met hers, sad but tough. Why not roam for a spell with a fellow canid, however strangely wrought by breeding? The kits didn't need her anymore, and to judge from the conversations she overheard at the coffee stand and the corn cooker, there was no reason not to enjoy life, fix herself up, deploy her remaining presentable features. Despite the mange, she was still trim around the flanks and had most of her teeth.

The dog didn't want to upset her, but how, exactly, did she lose her wagger? So that was it: this smooth pooch was just a sniffer-out of trauma tales, a freak-hound. She couldn't decide whether to ditch him, or tear his throat out.

"It's not a fetish," he said. "Docked or not docked, it doesn't matter. I'm not out to use you. If you look closely, you'll notice that I'm past all that nonsense myself."

They were sitting under the elevator shaft at Cal State, one of her favorite spots with a view of the river (her burrow visible near the Chinatown warehouses) and plentiful vermin in the ivy. Coyote wouldn't have minded, now that he mentioned it, but it looked like this was going to be all talk.

"Not necessarily," he said, beginning to groom around her ears. "I can't promise consistency, though. I have to go home to eat, and sometimes they lock me in the yard for days at a time."

III.

It happened out east of the rail yards, Coyote told him. She was pregnant, hunting rats in the dumpsters with the kits' father and some of his pack. At one point a lid came down, and she slowed her scramble to take the weight, letting the others escape as she strained to keep it aloft. It pinned her fast as she slithered out, half-hanging and half-perched on the metal catch-bar. She had just enough purchase to turn and gnaw at her tail until it came free.

"So you're loyal," the dog said. Coyote shrugged. He had no idea that in her wild youth she'd taken a bullet for a cougar, and didn't ask, didn't even seem curious about the paw. So many of the local dogs had gunshot wounds, it lacked the exotic flair of an all-night self-mutilation. But, sure, she'd admit that coyotes stuck together when they felt like it—at least that particular night the pack, seeing her predicament, silently watched as she freed herself, and then filed away into the night, her lover among them. That was as far as it went, though. After she dropped to the ground, eyes dim from the strain, and staggered off into the shadows, she looked around and found herself alone with her new body, an unfamiliar outline to fool the watchers, as the approaching trash truck slung metal down the street.

"I'm not sure I have the same definition of loyalty that you do," Coyote said. They led such different lives, finally. She'd traveled, she had seen the world from the tops of mountains and the edges of countless freeways, and loved a big cat. He'd never even eaten roadkill, and she could tell that the idea of sexual experimentation among the feliforms would turn him off. But he had a point. After tonight, he was her dog. She toyed with the idea of finding a bigger burrow but wasn't sure she could keep up with his needs. A healthy domesticated male, used to regular meals, could be more trouble than a litter of kits. Better he should maintain his independence, and she hers. He didn't propose anything radical, either, but showed her his neighborhood and a spot where she could curl up against the chain link along the alley, sheltered by an oleander, and they could at least talk. Coyote was skeptical.

"I'll send the neighborhood mutts into frenzies," she said, and sure enough, a bull terrier down the street went berserk as only a yard cur can. A light came on inside the house.

"That's my cue," the dog said. "It is what it is, but I'm solid, I hope you know that."

"You know where to find me," she said, and trotted off. This neighborhood gave her a bad feeling.

IV.

The big problem with cities is all the mental activity, Coyote decided, insomniac again and perched on a well-made travertine wall. It was early, still dark, with a hint of rain in the air and the Sunday crowds slumbering in their beds. She'd come to like museums, dodging security guards and cleaning crews, taking little naps in the sculpture gardens. She didn't know a thing about art, had no training at all, but just being in a place where almost everyone was thinking mostly about one thing, even empty, felt like a kind of respite. Omnivores can expect a lot from themselves, she decided. There's adaptability, and then there's losing sight of why you're even here, why life drags on so long, there's getting distracted by all the choices. Someone had dropped a scone into the landscaping, but she didn't feel hungry—she'd had it up to here with scones, frankly.

What did that dog see in her, anyway, he of the daily caresses, the full food dish, the standing appointment at the groomer? Like most of his kind, he was gregarious and trusting, laughing at her skittishness. If he were here, Coyote thought, he'd make a big game of this, want to romp and growl and bite neck on the travertine, and probably end up getting us kicked out. Still, Coyote knew she was made a certain way. She'd risk it, finally; she'd slink into that enemy-infested neighborhood and curl up next to the fence, ready for a warm breath of companionship—and why not, other than the inescapable fact that if she stayed more than a few minutes in that neighborhood, someone would shoot her? He was a nice dog.

A lone raven swooped onto a finial.

"There's a scone down there," she said. "I don't suppose it interests you."

"I was saving it for someone special," Coyote said. "Rough night?" The corvid, to be honest, wasn't looking so great.

"I flew into the side of a semi on the 405," Raven said, beginning her studied peck at the pastry. "We were a little buzzed. At least I didn't get hung up in the undercarriage, like some birds I could name."

Coyote had never seen her without the sidekick, come to think of it.

"I can't believe you're not eating this," Raven said.

"Aren't you sad at all? Won't you miss him?"

Raven looked at her with one eye, and went back to the scone. Coyote began to uncurl from her spot. It would be full daylight soon, time do some business.

"Work, work, work, Coyote," Raven said, rattling the empty paper. "Don't you ever get tired of chasing your tail?"

Coyote breathed, in and out, in and out, concentrating on the scent of wet scrub and trying to control her temper. Raven always managed to say something hurtful. Funny how she could be so philosophical about the thing with the dog, so resigned to the absolute doom that the relationship represented, but a stupid comment from a bird left her a little weepy.

"Sorry," Raven said. "That was thoughtless. But don't you miss it?"

Without waiting for an answer, she lifted off against the wind, and Coyote trotted past the gift shop, catching a glimpse of herself in a glass door. Certainly she was an oddity, nothing to brag about, asymmetrical with a vengeance. Coyote sniffed the air again. Someone down the hill was frying bacon, and it made her think. Corn sales tended to start slow in the forenoon. Maybe there was something else she could sell. Appetites abounded down there, for sure, posing the perennial omnivore's dilemma: which of several attractive options to choose. She swished into a culvert, just another brown-gray shadow, and she was gone.

RAVEN FORECLOSED

I.

She no longer looked like a bird with a future, even as she flew the usual transects. Instead of the concepts and patterns that normally kept Raven alive, she saw only something newly configured as the bottom, so near. She mentioned it to the mate at her shoulder, nearly blinded by the sun setting over the Pacific, and he cast an annoyed look her way: did he need to be alarmed by this, to take measures?

"If everything stays the same," she said as they pecked at cigarette butts along the Promenade, "if we go on like this month after month, does that sound like a cheerful prospect to you, or not?"

That kind of question can linger in the dead air between couples for years, until the times get hard and enforce any one of a number of changes. This was hard times, it turned out, and so instead of the cushy beach cities, abundant stale bagels at the craft trailers and shifting mosaics of barbecue leavings at the picnics of the Latin American diaspora, Raven found herself newly mateless once again, atop an old-fashioned telephone pole as the eastbound Greyhound sighed and disappeared down the frontage road. Depressed, she watched the trucks pass, sniffed the chemical stew rising off the lettuce fields. So this was Indio, gateway to the Coachella Valley. In the distance, a poisonous and beautiful body of water gleamed among the bathtub rings of the desert hills, where she would have to learn the subtleties of beached fish, of egret eggs and government corn, a new order of abundance.

II.

"It's all about frugality, about using the materials at hand to make a new start. Training and instinct can get us too specialized," Raven said as Magpie and Mockingbird fluffed their feathers in the sun.

"When the economy tanks, it's easy to get marooned," said Mockingbird, always a quick study. "Sure, there are grants and part-time gigs, but who would pay out the kind of money even one little bird needs for a Westside lifestyle?"

The wind ruffled the pages of a magazine Raven picked out of the trash: a retrospective of Dorothea Lange photographs opened at the Getty right after she left town.

"Now there's some real survivors," Mockingbird said. "The Madonna of the Plains, old hoboes with a single clean shirt and a sheaf of Wobbly propaganda in their knapsacks."

"What's a knapsack?" Magpie said.

"We're too effete for knapsacks." Raven took back the magazine. "Knapsacks represent a kind of competence that is alien to our kind. Honestly, I saw the most pathetic yard sales in West Hollywood and Culver City, IKEA bookshelves and espresso makers, exercise equipment, a whole catalogue of bad choices".

"Where'd all the money go to, I wonder," Mockingbird said.

"Too much credit," Magpie said. "No roots, no connections."

"You're a fine one to talk," Mockingbird said. "You're a total stray."

Raven tuned them out. Would she even be here, would she have escaped that sense of fatal drift if she'd persisted like so many others at the project of wanting, of considering colors, patterns, zoning variances, tile and bamboo, curtains and blinds?

Magpie was crying a little bit.

"You think it doesn't bother me?" She wiped her yellow eye. "That's what you think? It was such a crazy time. I hardly remember it, just some bad weather, a truck, the tomatoes. Tomatoes. Maybe I made some mistakes, maybe I got greedy..."

"Shut up," Raven said. "Don't go looking for pity around here."

She got ready to peck, but a man in torn jeans and a leather vest threw a broken board at her and she hopped away. Magpie and Mockingbird preened a little, and the leather vest man set a plate of hamburger in front of them.

"I remember your kind of bird," he said to Magpie. "Stockton, a thousand years ago."

"Mr. Futility," Raven said from her phone pole, "talking to you."

Magpie pecked at the hamburger.

"Nice," she said to Mockingbird. "Like sparrow chicks put through the blender."

"I've tried it before," Mockingbird said.

"He'll have you on cat food next," Raven screeched, laughing and lifting her wings.

"I'm happy to share," Magpie said. "Call it rent. I like the looks of that orange tree next to the trailer. No pecks while I'm sleeping, and I'll leave you each a third of this."

"Half for me," Raven said. "I am the bigger bird."

III.

Of the three of them, only Mockingbird was born there, but she said most of the natives acted pretty snobby, even to her.

"The owls are the worst, always going on about mice and lizards like they invented them. This kind of mouse, that kind of mouse."

"Mouse snobs, the worst," Raven said.

"If there's more wine," Magpie said, "I'll drink it."

"That and cheap hamburger." Raven poured her half a glass. Magpie gestured for her to fill it up.

"Was that a crack? He likes me, whatever. I remind him of better times. Is that so awful?"

"No one ever feeds a raven," Raven said. "Not even the tweakers of Imperial County."

"We're pretty lucky." Mockingbird was cheerful as usual. "Omnivores have it good. Did you read about those albatross babies, with their bellies full of plastic? And someone bulldozed the owl burrow right down the road, and I can't stop thinking about the poor fishing cormorants in Japan, I mean, it's total slavery."

Magpie served herself the last of the bottle.

"The world is private property," she lifted her glass to the other two, "and it all belongs to us. That's something, right?"

Raven snorted, which came out like a croak.

"No, really," Magpie said. "Look at yourself. You can outfly us, you can digest anything, that bill, my god, it's like a drill bit, nobody will ever, ever mess with you, Raven."

"Lunchtime," Mr. Futility said, setting a plate in front of Magpie and shooing Raven away. He pushed a chair into the shade and sat down heavily. His face had swollen in the past few days, his ankles so distended he wore flip-flops instead of his usual boots. Magpie pecked at the hamburger, peering around at the man in a way even Raven had to admit was charming. She hopped to the porch railing and strutted and groomed for a while so Raven could steal a few beaks full of hamburger. Magpie wasn't bad, Raven had to admit, like a grackle with looks and brains. But the wine was wearing her down. She stumbled on the porch railing, and her left wing trailed a bit.

IV.

"The problem with grackles," Mockingbird said, coming to rest on a stanchion below her, "is they never shut up."

"I've come to like it." Raven did, it wasn't a pose. The crepuscular racket of the grackles, and the deepening gold to the south, the dirty haze of irrigated agriculture and miles of windblown sediment, the peace, the sense of space, all made her think she could eventually adapt to her new life.

"You didn't grow up listening to the clacks and croaks all day long. It gets old."

"We didn't have them in Santa Monica, just seagulls and English sparrows like you wouldn't believe."

"Rotten Limeys," Magpie said, slurring her words.

"The sun sets so early after the time change," Mockingbird said. "We probably shouldn't be drinking all day"

"At least not this swill," Magpie said. "I heard there's a better selection at the Costco in Cat City, if we felt like making the trip."

"Who is this we? I'm the only one with any spare cash."

Raven flew away, feeling bitter. Mockingbird had all that talent and look at her, she was so easygoing compared to Magpie, who was, she'd admit, pretty, and exotic down here at least. But up north magpies were a dime a dance, and really the three of them came from the same place, avian trash, roadside breeds without much dignity. Terns dive for fish, the kestrels and owls hunt real living beasts, and we wait outside the truck stop for someone to drop his French fries, even the best of us sing to the speed freaks and the lettuce pickers for handouts.

Always with the self-loathing, Raven scolded herself.

V.

Raven flew over tamarisk and rabbitbrush, over unexploded ordnance and abandoned ashrams. A month or so in Mexico would clear her head, it had to, solitary contemplation of the fish farms and dirt roads of Santa Clara, maybe a trip out on the Sea of Cortez with the pangueros, some tacos and the smell of diesel and wood smoke. If nothing else, she could chill with Coyote's family for a while, she had addresses, the usual network of canids who cross at will, trip the sensors for fun, her kind, earthbound soul mates.

"Nothing's much fun anymore," one of Coyote's uncles told her. "Some real tough dogs came up from Sinaloa last year, and all of us amateurs got motivated to quit real quick."

The moon, waning gibbous, lay on its back over the sea, a hell of a sight.

"It'll be at the half tomorrow," said the old Coyote, not that it matters anymore. "I used to watch that old moon like some kind of Galileo, sister."

"Like an old smuggler, maybe," Raven said.

"Maybe."

"Is there any way to make money with the new guys?"

"A bird like you, with papers, no record, some Westside snazz, you kidding? Sure. There's dope, people going over wet, guns, dog fights, chicken fights, all kinds of money rackets. Some bad doings, Raven. I wouldn't want my girls mixed up in it."

"It beats going back to dullsville."

"If that's how you see it."

VI.

Raven sorted out the pile of pesos and dollar bills on the hood of Chavo's pickup truck. She was good at sorting out the crowd, too, figuring who was serious about betting and who got too excited or drunk to keep track, and she played it just straight enough to keep them happy, and just crooked enough to make Chavo money whatever happened in the pit.

She tried to avoid the roosters in their cages, not because they were crazy, but because they were so beautiful, and said such horrible things to her. Ignore them, Chavo told her, it gets them pumped for their fights.

It was Sunday night, and the Mexican Republic was officially 199 years and three days old. Chavo said they'd made more money that weekend than he had during Holy Week.

It was dark away from the pit and the groups of men showing off their birds. Raven and Chavo made their own party, a pint of Crown Royal, the fireworks just visible from Caborca. The band at the bar next door that played one bad ranchera song after another.

"My sister's kids went to Dolores Hidalgo on a school trip," Chavo said. "Where the revolution started. They hung Padre Hidalgo's head in a cage off the side of a building after they shot him. Nice history, huh?"

Raven sipped her whiskey and kept sorting the money. Chavo liked to talk, explain the bloodiness of Mexico's past, do a little amateur sociology. God, she was tired. She had a headache starting behind her eyes. She counted a stack of bills twice, then three times, and got a different amount each time.

"Chavito," she said, "I'm starting to lose it. I think I'm getting a migraine."

"Females. No stamina. Go on, go home. Here." He tossed her a bundle of twenties. "Don't puke on the money."

Raven hopped to a thicket of creosote and threw up. It didn't make her feel a bit better.

"Kill," said a faint voice by her. "Get out the cage and kill, kill."

Through the milky throb of a full-on migraine, Raven could just see a rooster, his chest bloodied and part of his crop visible through a slash in his neck. His claws twitched, and he stretched his beak as if to peck, then collapsed on his side.

"Whole life in a cage," the rooster gasped. "You wonder why I'm in a rage? Tell them, one time I was on a trustee crew, I shoved this homie Salvatore into the truck lane on the 60. Guy name Clarence is doing time for it. Never felt right about that."

"Settle down." Raven said.

"I know you, Morena. Ugly puta. If I wasn't disemboweled, I'd make you squawk, even if you are ugly."

"Be quiet."

"Nice way you earn your living, sister. Free-loader. Chingada."

He seemed to talk forever, saying the same foul

things over and over. Raven retched again. How long had she been in this roost? It was starting to get light, but it could just be the moon rising. She'd lost track of where it was, full or new, waxing or waning.

"Water," the rooster gasped.

"I could use some myself." Raven stopped to listen. Something was eating something, messily, on the other side of the creosote bush, and Raven hopped to the top of a cactus in quick panic as a mean-looking dog brought his teeth down on the half-dead rooster. Three or four more of last night's losers lay dismembered and scattered in the gray morning light, blood and bronze and iridescent green feathers bright amid the rocks. A nice way to earn a living, that dead gallito was right. Raven felt weak from her bad night, but calm, more grounded than usual, ready to decide some things. She spotted the rising equinoctial sun off her right shoulder and set off for the north.

VII.

"What happened to this place? It's trashed. Is the trailer totally gone?"

"Someone towed it off, what was left of it," Mockingbird said. "Didn't you know?"

"I was in Mexico."

"Way to say something before you leave. We wondered. It happens once in a while, when these guys get careless. Who cares? He was sick anyway."

Mockingbird stifled a sob.

"What is wrong with you?"

"Michael Jackson died."

Raven snorted. "Like, months ago, Mockingbird. Where have you been?"

"Oh, you know how summer is, you have chicks, it's all crickets, crickets, spiders, grasshoppers, crickets, always watching for raccoons, worrying about everything, and then they get so ugly for a while, so demanding, such brats. There's no time to think, or look at a newspaper, or anything, and then they're gone and it's even worse, too quiet. I've been just really feeling sad, he was really a part of my life for a while, you know?"

"Forget about Michael Jackson. I can't believe Mr. Futility is dead."

"They said you could see the fire all the way to Niland."

"How did Magpie take it?"

"She's under the orange tree."

Raven hopped to the tree to examine the heap of feathers, the cracked yellow bill, a few tardy ants marching around.

"She totally let herself go," Mockingbird said. "Wine every night, pills, whatever she could find, and no eating, of course. She tangled with a couple of cats, couldn't spot trouble anymore. This wasn't her world."

"Couldn't someone talk to her?"

"You could have, I think. You're pragmatic that way. Those cats never came around when you were here, believe me. Everyone figured she'd pull herself together and fly back where she belonged. But I think she really cared about him."

Raven tossed the iridescent feathers, not sure why she did it, mixing them with the dead leaves and dirt. This was great, run from one heap of dead bird matter to another, borrow trouble and carry the debt wherever she went.

"You look great, really," Mockingbird said. "Mexico agrees with you. It's getting very fun and crazy around here, some Canada geese came in yesterday and there are parties every night. You always show up when things start happening, Raven."

"No parties," Raven said. "I'm ready to tone it down a little."

"You?" Mockingbird screeched a little, tossed herself into the air and ate a mosquito. "Some PBS and early to bed? You're a riot, Raven. You'll never tone it down."

Raven hopped once, flapped once, and she was on top of her phone pole again. Shotguns popped in the distance. Stupid Mockingbird had no idea why the parties over there were so good, but Raven had seen it all, on her way north she'd perched on the blinds and the cleaning stations, watched the florid men in full camo load innocent-looking coolers into the trucks and sampled what they left behind. It was tempting to tell Mockingbird all of this, but Raven watched her for a while, hunting and flashing her dark gray and white pattern, showing a hint of yellow in the right light, tuning up a bit as dusk fell. Why abuse her for what she couldn't see?

"Don't get all pissy and fly away, Raven. You always do that. At least if you're here, you know it can't get any worse."

"It can always get worse," Raven said. "I will spare you the details. Oh, there go the grackles. I love the grackles."

"Grackles appear reliably at dusk," Mockingbird said. "If that makes you happy, you'll always be happy. Lucky Raven."

It was cold enough, or almost, for a triple cognac. Heron, always satisfied and never satisfied, let the wind caress the feathers atop his head. Even without his black breeding plumes he looked so elegant, reflected in the afternoon gloom, distorted just a bit by the brackish water at his feet. His markings gave him an old-world appeal. No one had to tell him that. No one had to tell him anything. Once in a great while the urge to mate came over him, but mostly lately just a diffused panic in his blood, early in the morning, late afternoon, whenever he let his guard down a bit. Today he could feel it coming on, maybe best to sit with it, see where it took him. He hated that feeling, the out-of-control agitation. What lay behind it? He tried to stand steady against the tide of anxiety. The swamp, after all, the ocean past the swamp, the few weathered gray houses and one raw new one, all looked the same as ever. This terrible sensation, it turned out, didn't change the look or smell or sound of his surroundings, didn't turn the world inside out, only made everything insufferably strange. So this is what it is like to experience some disease that is entirely mental, he thought. It would be good, maybe, to talk to another heron about it, learn if this was unique to him, but herons don't do that, especially in these mistrustful times, shrinking estuaries, dwindling numbers of suitable perches and fish. Maybe it was his imagination, but even the fingerlings he still caught, even the frogs and crayfish, the aquatic larvae and water bugs, tasted funny, like some essential nutrient had gone missing, the mineral trace of uninterrupted bog no longer fed the estuary, too many plastics, hydrocarbon residues, something.

Anxiety made him irritable and defensive, and this heron hardly felt disposed to apologize for it. Who could say what the future held, but he for one didn't have any more illusions. He could rely on a steady income that, okay, maybe depended a little more on the market than was prudent, but otherwise he owed nothing and expected nothing.

How long had it been this way? It came on so gradually. When he first found the perch, it looked at first like the perfect place for some good, deep thinking, maybe a big creative project, some kind of web thing, why not? He had good, if superficial, relationships with a couple of females upstream, one knew more about movies and wine than he did, and miracle of miracles, wasn't smug or butch about it. Maybe it was the comfortable relationships to blame, actually, that distracted him just enough. The weeks slipped away. He at least had it enough on the ball to notice when the thing with the females started to sour, when the conversation turned once too often to the future, to his stock portfolio, plans to remodel, god forbid. He'd done that a few times, long ago, he'd served his time.

But nest building wouldn't have been as scary as his latest habit. Where do these ideas come from, what chemical imbalance, or just boredom, drove him to venture early every morning across the estuary to the brand new back yard of the redwood monstrosity scarring the middle of his territory? His incursions, even the early, tentative ones, had a serious undertone of contempt. If you're going to build a pond and stock it with expensive carp, he silently lectured the owner, you might want to talk to someone who knows about ciconiiformes before you dig.

Rather than dig into his capital, Heron rode out the slump working a few hours a week at a friend's wine store, a place so exclusive you had to know what you wanted before anyone would even talk to you. The shop operated under a business plan buried far underneath multiple layers of exclusivity and felt more like a private club or someone's living room than a retail outlet. Pity the poor visitor, glassy-eyed and bloated from a lifetime of Trader Joe's plonk and robo-chicken, who might wander in ready to drop a bit of holiday cash on a nice bottle. Heron didn't hesitate to run a black beady eye from the tip of their 20-dollar haircut to the hem of the inevitable elastic-eased denim shorts and deploy his head-feathers to suggest refined contempt. If they persisted, he always had a few bottles ready to unload on rubes with no palate, Chileans and Australians Paul had gambled on not wisely and not well, overpriced oddities from big-name vineyards that hadn't moved among the people who knew something about the merely decent, the great, and the difference between the two.

Instead of going to the carp banquet and pissing off the locals, he should do a few laps around the duck pond and then stick his head in the door at the wine shop like a good bird. He lifted himself into the air, across the highway and toward the airstrip, made a few low passes to give the Cessnas a thrill. No one could persuade him that the stiff, passive things on the tarmac didn't react to a real flyer.

"Inanimate, Heron, for sure," Duck said.

"I don't know," Heron said. "They kind of look like you. Fly like you, too."

He could talk like this with Duck, as they stood on the bank drying off and preening a bit after their workout. How long had they known each other, after all, watched the sparrows fight and the gulls race each other almost every day since they'd fledged. Talking to Duck showed that Heron hadn't lost touch with his roots, at least not completely.

"You should stay away from that fishpond." Duck flicked a Tostitos bag into the shallows. "They've laced it with something."

"Probably just for the algae."

"Still. Might shrink your pecker."

"Plenty to spare. Anyway, they could stand to do something about the algae here. These rocks smell like a landfill."

"What are you talking about? Fresh midwinter algae is very good for you."

Heron gulped down a couple of minnows instead and took off, elegantly, just to show Duck how it could look without the heaviness, the unsightly splashing around. Now to show up on a Wednesday afternoon in

January, a gift to Paul, who could have expressed a little gratitude instead of keying himself out of the computer without a word and pointing to the bread tray they kept at the tasting counter. It was all greasy crumbs of cheese crackers and breadstick shards.

"That looks pretty trashy," Heron said.

"It's why I hire you," Paul said, and before Heron could remind him exactly what kind of business arrangement they had and how little commission Heron could expect to earn on a slow winter weekday, he was gone, barely bothering to hold the door for the wispy blonde in cloth slippers who ducked in under his arm.

The girl wanted a bottle for her dad's birthday, a nice red, not too heavy. She didn't know shit about wine.

"How much do you want to spend?"

"Fifty bucks should do it, right? I'll go up a little more if you'll promise not to say the word 'drinkable,' or compare it to something inedible, like leather."

People who were sick of wine snobs annoyed Heron almost as much as full-on wine snobs, but he found himself pulling some pretty nice bottles off the shelf.

"Oh, confusing. Stop," she said. "What do you drink?"

"Honestly," Heron said, "I'm pretty much exclusively into brown liquors right now. Cognac, balsams, really old bourbons, stuff like that."

"Do you sell those here?"

"No. You have to go into the city."

"The city?"

"A city. Some large city, including the one near us."

"Okay, yeah. The Bay Area self-regard gets old, kind of."

Heron shrugged in a way he knew made him seem dismissive, full of himself. So what? He was a heron, and he worked in a wine shop. Why buck the stereotype?

Paul came back while he was finishing up the sale. Heron as usual noted the broken veins in his nose, the fretful way he started trying to do all of his business at once, unpacking a shipment, thumbing through invoices, twitching a barrel from one side of the tasting bar to another. He disappeared into the back, finally, and Heron wrapped the bottle in newspaper and handed it to the girl.

"No little gift bag?"

"We have them, but they're vulgar. This is our old-world touch."

"You look familiar," the girl said. "Someone's been messing around our fish pond, but I'm sure he's younger. Is he related to you?"

"Me? A respectable heron, with a job?"

"A job, and a boyfriend, maybe a Weimaraner?"

Heron made a buzzing sound.

"Wrong again. No boyfriend, no dog. Not my style."

"Anyway, my dad says he's going to shoot that heron if it keeps eating his carp."

Heron shrugged again.

"Maybe it's one of my old girlfriends, they're all so

bitter. Say, how many square feet is that place, anyway?"

"About eight thousand, not including the garage."

"Garage plural, you mean. Just for the two of you?"

"I have a couple of half-brothers who spend summers. Are you trying to guilt me? Get in line. My dad's an oligarch and I'm doing a grad degree in conservation biology. Nobody approves of anybody in my world."

The bell on the door rang and Paul came out from the storeroom.

"So did the little hippie actually buy anything?"

"You have 80 bucks in the drawer that weren't there a half hour ago."

Heron stared past him without realizing he was doing it, a habit. Paul moved his head around to show how he was making eye contact.

"Heron, Jesus. Do you ever get tired of yourself?"

"What do you mean?"

"I mean do you get tired of being you?"

"I like being me."

"That's a problem."

"Paul, are you firing me?"

"No, no, anyone who can sell an eighty-dollar bottle of wine to a kid who looks like she sleeps under the freeway is officially unfireable."

"Her house, Paul? That crazy custom job on Stephens Marsh."

"See? You can call them."

"The guy put in a fish pond. Who builds a pond

when he already lives on a marsh?"

"What do you think of this door chime?" Paul took down the abalone shells he'd brought from Mexico. "It seems a little much, all of a sudden."

If I keep going this way much longer, Heron thought as he flew back across the highway, Paul will end up thinking he's my boyfriend. This is not a result, he told himself sternly, you should find acceptable.

Really, he had everything he wanted. He'd planned for this, enough income to keep him, almost, and acreage, lots of it. Someday it would be worth more than that software millionaire's white elephant, all he had to do was sit and wait, and he had plenty of practice there. Why, then, instead of practicing his famous patience, did he fly past his welcoming perch and drop to the edge of the carp pond again? This was worse than the brandy. A yellow light glowed from an upstairs window, a big temptation. He could just hop to that little dormer and ...

There she sat, playing around with a laptop computer and, was that a turntable? He knew the type. She'd have some Thoreau on the bookshelf, a lot of John Muir she hadn't read (who could?) and something by that tree-sitter girl, Julia Butterfly whatever, she'd have read the first chapter.

"Isn't it a little early in the year for you to be following me around?"

Heron jumped. God, he was so not sharp lately, total

coyote-bait if he didn't watch it.

"You know, the coastal microclimates, warm winters, we're pretty much ready whenever," Heron said. "How'd Papa like the wine?"

"More than the i-gadget his girlfriend got him. She was pissed."

"I should meet him sometime."

"Honestly, no. The only interaction he wants with you is through the wrong end of a Bushmaster. He has it loaded with birdshot. You ate his favorite carp."

"Swear not." Heron searched his memory. "A carp, I'd remember. I may have snacked on a couple of mosquito fish or a frog, but there are tons."

"Okay, another heron, then. The younger one."

He felt the blood start to pound in his head. Another heron on his property? Intolerable.

"Maybe it was a raccoon."

"Dad saw you, okay? With a ten-inch carp in your bill, flying west. Do you know how much that fish was worth?"

"He should shoot the idiot who designed his pond. If they're built right, we can't get at the carp."

"He did it himself, and he's super proud of it. See why you two shouldn't discuss this?"

The girl paused. A V of geese flew overhead. Where could they be going in mid-January? Everything was so weird lately. It was dark, cold. The damp breathed out of the marsh like a living thing. Heron straightened his neck, pointed his bill to the sky, and made a clacking sound.

"I guess that means you want to come in," the girl said, and opened the window.

It was unlike anything Heron had ever experienced before. She made him wait—I know about you birds, quick on the trigger, she said—and do unfamiliar things to parts of her body totally uninvolved with the matter at hand. At some point she got out an old Polaroid camera and took pictures that developed with odd gold splotches in the corners—the film itself was old, she said, hard to find.

"If you ever see Polaroid film, like at a yard sale, call me right away. This stuff went through the x-ray at the airport, see how it spoiled?"

She pointed at the corner of the photograph with a clinical finger, as if it didn't show her thin legs tangled with his spread wings, something out of a pervert's idea of art nouveau, a pornographic cabaret dancer or conjurer's assistant. She took out a red Sharpie and drew harlequin diamonds around the border, then glued the photo to a branch of driftwood. She had piles of nature junk in her room, manzanita branches with pink, peeling bark, dried bulbs of kelp sprinkled with silver glitter, and the largest collection of fake tattoos he'd ever seen.

"I could put one on your thigh," she said. "Maybe a mermaid?"

"Too human." Now that his pulse had calmed down, he didn't bother hiding the aloof look anymore. He'd regret those photos for sure.

"That's not a very gentlemanly comment," the girl said. "It's late, anyway."

Heron stood on the dormer trying to collect himself. He needed a glass of something strong, some fish, something to replace the minerals he'd just sweated out. Sex that fancy is a bad idea for a creature with a low startle point. He hopped down to the carp pond, littered with the owner's efforts at deterrence: a tangled black net, a heron statue, a fake alligator. The water looked ugly, glowing with a chemical sheen, and through the pre-dawn fog Heron could see the stiff orange bodies floating on the top, the plastic jug of pesticide half sunk in the rushes and flags planted along the shallow end. He looked around. They couldn't blame him for this, surely.

"It was an accident," a scruffy young heron said, stepping out of the shadows. "I was watching the show in that upstairs window, and my foot must have slipped."

"So did your bill," Heron said, looking at the yellow bottle more closely. "It looks like you gouged a few holes before you tipped it over."

"Someone like you," the younger heron sounded close to tears, "you don't even bother to hide what a jerk you are, how you have, like, nothing to offer her, you're proud of it."

Heron began to argue, surprised that he was even bothering to answer this punk, but before he could make his point he heard the dry click of a magazine being shoved into place and plunged into the marsh ahead of a burst of gunfire. The other bird stood there, staring up at the yellow window, but Heron didn't wait to see what would happen next.

"What kills me," Heron said the next day, grubbing a stubborn mite from under his wing, "is how the survival instinct was just gone in that heron."

"We're getting it, too," Duck said. "Degeneracy. You'll see ducklings barely fledged, sitting around the boat ramp, huffing the antifreeze puddles."

They stood for a while, letting the wind dry their feathers.

"So," Duck said. "Will you try to see her again?"

"Ask me when I recover," Heron said. "She nearly killed me."

"Get it while you can. There's a for-sale sign on that place, did you see?"

"Since when?"

"This morning. Blue Heron Realty, high-end properties exclusively. How about that? He'll never get his price in this market."

Another heron dropped from the sky to the opposite end of the duck pond. It was the scruffy kid, unscathed. Duck waited for Heron to lose it and chase him away.

"What is this," Duck finally said, "a budding bromance? The beginning of a beautiful friendship?"

"Hate the game, not the player," Heron said. "We've been through some things."

The kid across the pond drew one leg up and closed his eyes. Heron sighed and did the same. He braced for the usual flurry of panic that so often hit him when he got ready to sleep, but it didn't come. Fifteen years on this earth, nearly his life expectancy. How many nest mates did he have to shove to the ground to get here?

"Hey," he shouted across the pond. The kid opened one eye. "How did that carp taste?"

"Couldn't get it down," the kid shouted back. "Too big. I forgot the half-the-length-of-the-bill rule. Gave it to a raccoon."

"Look. Take her a pile of sticks or something. Females like that."

"You think I don't know? Shut up and let me sleep."

Duck cocked his head, rolled his eyes, and swam away. Heron shook his feathers. Not bad for a bird still in winter plumage. His moods were his moods, but nothing said he couldn't splash out once in a while.

DUCK GETS IT DONE

Things had been going well for Duck. Today he had friends over, in the garden, which he insisted on calling the garden even though he was in America, where people called it "the yard," and he was himself American. He'd read a lot, though, during a sabbatical year with a grant, one round of exquisiteness after another. With support like that, he could really feel like an artist people took seriously, someone with something to offer.

Tina was an artist, too, or kind of. They'd trained together, she and Duck, and she still painted, played the piano, did what she could steal from the day job she had to take, finally, because of her bad habits. Her worst habit, she joked, was alienating people, but everyone agreed, including Duck, that her real problem was crudity, a kind of tone-deafness, a tendency to provoke reactions. Still, she didn't take the air out of the room like her new friend. Duck was pouring tea, pouring wine, trying not to react to Renate's comments.

"Your problem," Renate was saying, and how dare she identify his problem already after meeting him, what, once, at a dinner? "...your problem is that you're an idealist, you want everything to work and make sense and be beautiful," and she rambled on for a while about how her cousins ran an auto shop in Santiago that wasn't really an auto shop, but some kind of contingent enterprise based on reselling imported auto parts to the police and military. Not that he tried too hard, but Duck got lost in all the contingencies and nuances. She had a point with all of this, a personal theory about accepting imperfection and recognizing that not everyone had the luxury of insisting that things work out properly or even...but here he lost her again and she got offended. She had an appointment and she'd grab a bus to the Mission, no need for Tina to run her around on a Saturday afternoon.

The gate slammed and Duck waited for the inevitable question.

"So, do you like her?" and without waiting for an answer, "She's kind of intense, but that's what I need, someone to jolt me out of my patterns."

"I suppose if you have a tough day at work, she can at least tell you how much worse the juvenile justice system is in Chile."

"It is crazy-bad, you're right, but at least there's usually extended family to take a kid with problems at home."

"Not here?"

"God no. Nothing we can rely on. Sometimes it's fine, more often it's generations of complete dysfunction. But crap. What I really want to do is play. Do you mind? Your piano is so much better than mine."

She stayed most of the afternoon, messing around with some ragtime, some Satie, mashing them up, until Renate texted her for a ride home.

He liked so many things about Tina. She didn't catch sarcasm, didn't get her feelings hurt, didn't have to resist a negative comment by knowing agreement and then the stupid blue-skying people felt like they had to do lately. Duck was tired of hearing about the world from the self-important migratory types all around him. What's the point of paying the insane rents we pay, he said, if we're always flying away for half a year at a time?

He knew he shouldn't, but he fussed around for too

long, fluffing and picking and making a mental list of what bugged him about Renate. One: she was "creative," a writer, but didn't seem to finish anything. Two: she was political in a way that seemed to demand something from him. Three: she didn't like him, she didn't look at him when she talked, she looked either at Tina or at a space just to the right of him. She seemed to think he was complacent, she scorned the garden and the place on the water and the decent bottles Heron cut him deals on. He was a homebody, he even missed Heron and the old pond sometimes, but had to agree that a city was better for him, more stimulation. Those small Central Coast towns, if you aren't careful, you agree to teach a couple of classes at the art co-op, then show a couple of pieces at the galleries, maybe they give you a name exhibit with nice card-stock posters all over town, and the next thing you know you're one of the watercolor crowd.

He had a couple of hours of light left, so he went to the shoreline and started moving some sticks into piles. It always calmed him to just mess around in the mud with his materials during the golden hour, use the tactile intelligence that never let him down. He tried to ignore the couple on the bank with binoculars.

"What is that?"

"Just a mallard with some weird mongrel markings."

"What is he doing?"

"Who knows? Behavior. They're so debased, living in town like this, they have no real instincts anymore."

"Hmmm...what's that? Something a little different?"

Oh, great. Duck knew that tone. He turned to look. A slender black-and-white bird sat miserably on the edge of a rotting dock. The birdwatchers were already huddled over their phones, identifying the stray. Arctic tern? Should we call it in? Go ahead, Duck said. Call it in, you nerdniks. Bring out the hordes. Dealing with the occasional rare bird alert was part of the deal, but it sucked anyway.

"Pochemu, Pochemu, hvers vegna." the bird mumbled thickly. Arctic tern indeed. Dang. That would mean a real invasion of earnest types in khaki vests. Life lists, year lists, county lists, state lists, world lists...

What did he care if Tern felt sick, worse than she'd ever felt before, like a hangover and a case of jet lag all rolled into one. Was this senility, finally? Was she terminal? How had she gone so far off course? She normally saw nothing below her but tundra, ice, and ocean, and the refineries and cities of Alameda County had her spinning.

Duck didn't know what happened, but he just lost it, swam in circles, shouting "ömurlegur fugl, zachvatchik, bad night, huh, you black-capped Eurotrash, you should have stayed away from the vodka." He even threw sticks, although he knew as he was throwing them that it was too theatrical, nyekulturny as Tern herself would have told him if she could have dredged up a riposte. He worked himself up and then had to go sit for a while, trying to get hold of himself and recollect the way he'd felt when the day was still peaceful, in the pond with the sticks, before Renate had shown up.

He should call Tina. She had the social worker's calming voice ready to deploy; he'd ask her to use it on him, like a dose of aural Haldol, but when she picked up she sounded frazzled.

"I'm waiting for Renate outside the Que Tal. She's really mad at me for some reason, I guess I was supposed to come and get her here and not at the hair salon, she was meeting people here? Duck, do you remember her saying anything like that? Oof, there's a text coming in, maybe it's her. Can I call you later?"

Duck heard a soft squawk from the bushes. Tern, of course. The best thing that bird could do was die right away, before the fleets of Subaru station wagons started to appear.

He knew all he needed to about these birds—the incredible stamina, the loyalty to the upper arctic, the slow mating cycle, the long lifespan—and frankly it made him sick, how stupidly delicate some species were, how the minute things warmed up a degree or two they completely lost their ability to cope and became someone's problem.

But it wasn't Tern. Another black-and-white bird, my god, was everyone going to bail out at his pond? Gulls and terns never hung out here, especially not these aerodynamic ocean-going types. Wait. Duck blinked.

"Aren't you...?"

The other bird didn't say anything. Maybe it couldn't. A Lesser Black-backed gull in these parts might as well have been from outer space.

"Hey!"

The gull turned to Duck, an expression of despair on his face. He half-opened his bill, and then went blank again.

"It must have been blowing like hell out there," Duck said. He swam in circles for a few minutes, thinking. Those birdwatchers didn't seem all that experienced, but the heavies were already showing up, with powerful telescopes and a lifetime of waiting for a Black-backed gull in their backyard. No way they'd miss two exotics, one of them a very big deal. He grabbed a surprised school of mosquito fish in his bill as he swam past and dumped them on the dock in front of the tern.

"Eat these, then fly into those bushes over there," he said. "Can you do that?"

Tern looked at him with dull eyes. She'd been epically lost before, it was part of the deal, but at this point she felt entirely too old for this, certainly too old to trust this garish duck, talking too loud and dumping these weird unwholesome-looking tadpole thingies in front of her. Still....

She tried one. They weren't bad.

"Eat," Duck said. "Eat, eat. Pakushet. Go on. Can you fly? Don't just nod, say something. Go on, fly over there.

There's another black-and-white larid over there, a tovar-ich. Don't freak out."

"I don't freak out, as you say," Tern said, and took off into the bushes. The birdwatchers dropped their phones and books and snapped their binoculars to their eyes, following her flight. Duck swam in a deceptively calm figure eight to the bushes himself. It would be dark soon. He'd wait until the crowd left, make the refugees stay out of sight until it was safe, and guide them to some remote rock off Marin. He was up to the challenge. If I have to, he said to himself grimly, I'll swim them out to the Farallones, I'll feed them the entire way, whatever dis-gusting mollusk they fancy.

It wasn't self-interest, he told Tina a week later, exhausted in her living room, letting her comb the sand out of his feathers. Renate was gone, and that was a relief, for Tina too, she admitted. It wasn't altogether altruism either.

"You aren't used to these mixed feelings," Tina said. "It shows in your work. It's so clean, so peaceful."

"I value my peace and quiet, sure. But you should have seen that gull. He was stoic. The tern, too. It's like they both just hunkered down and waited for the worst to happen. I don't get it. I've never admired stoicism. Maybe I'm just too rosy-rosy, but it seemed wrong to let things unfold, not give them a chance to get better." He fluffed and shook. "Did you get it all? I hate sand."

Tina stopped combing and they watched the light

change to the north.

"Things have been going well for you," Tina said.

"Why shouldn't they?"

To Les

CONTENTS

1   Bad Habitats

9   Cougar Comes of Age

21   Coyote in Winter

33   Raven Foreclosed

47   Big Cranky

61   Duck Gets It Done

ABOUT THE AUTHOR

Alisa Slaughter has published fiction and creative non-fiction in several literary journals, including *Santa Monica Review*, *The Missouri Review*, *Natural Bridge*, *Alimentum*, and *SundaySalon.org*. She lives in the mountains of Southern California.

COLOPHON

Bad Habitats
© 2012 Alisa Slaughter

ISBN: 978-1-938900-04-4

Library of Congress Control Number: 2013933002

Winner of the 2012 Gold Line Press Chapbook Competition in Fiction

"Cougar Comes of Age" and "Coyote in Winter" appeared previously in *Santa Monica Review*, issues 18:1 (Spring, 2006) and 21:1 (Spring, 2009).

Special thanks to *SMR* editor Andrew Tonkovich for his guidance and support.

A version of "Raven Fore-closed," was broadcast on *Bibliocracy Radio*, KPFK Los Angeles, on August 1, 2012.

"Bad Habitats" appeared in *Miss Leslie's Magazine* February, 2013.

Thanks also to L'a.i.r. de Fez in Fez, Morocco, AiR le Parc in Pampelonne, France, and the University of Redlands.

Printed by BookMobile in the United States of America

Design: Becca Abbe
Gold Line Press Logo: Nicholas Katzban

Gold Line Press publishes chapbooks of poetry and fiction with the aim to promote the work of emerging writers as well as showcase the chapbook form. The goal of our annual competition is to support exceptional writers through the publication and broad distribution of their work. Gold Line Press is associated with the University of Southern California's Ph.D. program in Literature and Creative Writing.

3501 Trousdale Parkway
THH 431
Los Angeles, CA 90089
www.goldlinepress.com